P. Crumble and Jonathan Bentley

We Are All BRAVE

An Omnibus Book from Scholastic Australia

We are all **BRAVE**

I'll speak up for you.

When you are hurting,

I'm feeling it too.

We are all BRAVE

We all make mistakes.

Saying you're sorry

might be all it takes.

We are all **BRAVE**

It's fine to say no.

Your voice will be heard;

let your feelings show.

We are all **BRAVE**

Things come to an end.

There's no easy way

to farewell a friend.

We are all **BRAVE**

Life's not a contest.

Be your true self

and you'll live your life best.

We are all **BRAVE**

Go try something new!

You might discover

a new point of view.

We are all **BRAVE**

We have doubts within.

Give life your best shot;

do not let fear win.

We are all **BRAVE**

The world can be dark.
Do not let the gloom
dim your bright spark.

We are all **BRAVE**

Show love every day.

Don't live to regret

the words you don't say.

We are all **BRAVE**

You might miss your goal.

There are things in life

we cannot control.

We are all **BRAVE**
Be fearless and loud.
Defend what is right
and live your life proud!

For Benny and Margot, for embracing new beginnings with enthusiasm and love—PC

For Harvey and Ffion—JB

Omnibus Books
an imprint of Scholastic Australia Pty Limited
PO Box 579 Gosford NSW 2250
ABN 11 000 614 577
www.scholastic.com.au

Part of the Scholastic Group
Sydney · Auckland · New York · Toronto · London · Mexico City · New Delhi · Hong Kong · Buenos Aires · Puerto Rico

Published by Scholastic Australia in 2024.

ISBN 978-1-76152-465-3

A catalogue record for this book is available from the National Library of Australia

Typeset in Austral Slab.

Printed in China by RR Donnelley.

Scholastic Australia's policy, in association with RR Donnelley, is to use papers that are renewable and made efficiently from wood grown in responsibly managed sources, so as to minimise its environmental footprint.

10 9 8 7 6 5 4 3 2 25 26 27 28 29 / 2